T

Also published by Patrick Hunt

Caravaggio 2004
House of the Muse 2005
Rembrandt 2006
Alpine Archaeology 2007
Ten Discoveries That Rewrote History 2007
Myths for All Time 2007
Renaissance Visions: Myth and Art 2008
Poetry in the Song of Songs 2008
Cloud Shadows of Olympus 2009
Myth and Art in Ekphrasis 2010
Puer Natus Est: Art of Christmas 2011
Dante's Inferno: Critical Insights 2012
Wine Journeys: Myth and History 2013

A Few Hundred Thoughts

Selected Aphorisms and Fabulae of Patrick Hunt

Patrick Hunt

Pirene Press

First published in the United States of America in 2013
by Pirene Press, an imprimatur of the Corinthian Publishing Group,
San Francisco, California

Library of Congress Cataloging in Publication data

Hunt, Patrick N.,
    A Few Hundred Thoughts/Patrick Hunt
    Selected Aphorisms and Fabulae of Patrick Hunt

ISBN – 978-0-578-13533-5

Typeset in Garamond

Printed and bound in the United States

        www.pirenepress.com
        www.corinthianpress.com

This little compendium is dedicated to

John D. Gibbon,

Mathematician,

John Perry,

Philosopher,

& James Geary,

Poet and Aphorist

Preface & Acknowledgments

Greek property in ancient society was often marked out by a boundary pillar, a *horos* stone that set up a determined space. [1] One word for the act of marking exact boundaries was *'aphorízein* ("to mark off by boundaries, to set bounds, to define"). Derived in part from this Greek verb, an aphorism is a pithy saying, conveying defined truth in a tightly determined construction of a few words whose boundaries were set by verbal economy and precision. [2] Although they can be somewhat different expressions, aphorisms, proverbs, maxims, apothegms and epigrams are the result of taut distillation, yielding truths or surprises in a few words. While maxims tend to illustrate principles or rules, appearing didactic or asking for moral agreement, apothegms tend to be cynical, expressing a dour outlook. When it is sympotic, a reminder of human ephemerality and the need to examine and appreciate life, such wisdom in a few words is also often moralistic. Most descriptions of aphorisms and the like agree they are mini-poems, striving for maximum punch in minimum words, a kind of intellectual judo.

For perfection, Virgil's profound poetic golden lines come to mind. Here intense condensation in writing, honing and polishing over a considerable time crystallizes his art

---

[1]   J. Ober. "Greek Horoi: Artifactual Texts and the Contingency of Meaning", in D. B. Small, ed. *Methods in the Mediterranean: Historical and Archaeological Views on Texts and Archaeology*. Leiden: E. J. Brill, 1995, 91 & ff.

[2]   H. G. Liddell and R. Scott, *Greek-English Lexicon*, Oxford: Clarendon Press, 1996, 292; *Oxford English Dictionary*. Oxford University Press, 1971, 384.

into gems. Even though his many facets of deliberate multiple ambiguities lend themselves intentionally to changing meanings at different readings, Virgil's golden lines are about as immortal as anything humans produce, and rarely does a translation do them any justice. The prophet Isaiah said that God's thoughts are so much higher than our thoughts, they are as high as the heavens are above the earth. The implication is that if we try to rethink God's thoughts, it may likely elevate the quality of our thinking. Whether philosophical, humorous, gnomic, literary or merely playful, good aphorisms are rich treasures to be mined. One of the most appropriate biblical proverbs is *Proverbs* 25:11: "A word fitly spoken is like apples of gold in frames of silver."

What makes an aphorism or maxim memorable is mostly indefinable but we know it when we see one that strikes us. Often it is the laconic truth pruned down to its lowest common denominator that is striking. On the one hand if the paring down or refining is too austere, we can lose the originality of thought or are left with an inexplicable riddle. On the other hand, balancing economy of words with connotative flavor where every word matters in exactly the right order with careful syntax is also critical. Whether ironic, subtle, biting, tongue in cheek, double entendre or paradox, the genre of an aphorism likely matters less if it brings a wry smile and some level of agreement even when provocative. Many aphorisms are word plays, also sharing euphony in similar or pleasing sounds; others are peripeties and antitheses with surprising reversals of expectation. In short, aphorisms share elements of poetry found in every language, ancient and modern. A sampling of aphorists may be illuminating. Juvenal and Voltaire play on sarcasm and hyperbole, Montesquieu probes with terse political analysis, Nietzsche and Kafka use poetic parable on one hand or veiled sophistry on the other. Pascal soars in realms of metaphysics but can bring us down to earth in a hurry. Oscar Wilde mocks with acerbic social commentary. After millennia Confucius remains the master of paradox. Precision and economy of thought are always desirable in writing in any literary form, although not easily mastered.

On the other hand, not so concise, a *fabula* is a different vehicle of thought. In a venerable literary genre using fictional stories, *fabulae* are more or less philosophical or moral parables casting improbable realities often in disguise. A literary form related to *fabula* is extended apologue, an old figure of Classical allegory. It helps to remember that both our common words "fable" and "fabulous" are derived from *fabula*. Ancient *fabulae* are often clothed in animal tales like the Aesopic originals or possibly ancient Egyptian illustrated animal stories, which La Fontaine later adapted into French. Humorous Medieval and Renaissance fabulae are well represented in Rabelais. Voltaire used the extended *fabula* to apply his Enlightenment humanism in *Candide* and *Zadig*. *The Adventures of Baron Munchausen* and to some extent *Simplicissimus* are also expressions of this genre. While Kafka excelled at such *fabulae* as conundrums, some C.S. Lewis writings as his Narnia tales and theological forays like *The Great Divorce* also fall into the category of extended *fabula*. Several of my original *fabulae* here have a fair share of historical allusions while offered as a motley sort of philosophical parables: "Alexander and the Caladrius", "The Museum of Ordinary Objects" and "The Wine of Rilke"; perhaps historically philosophical and more subtly parabolic than I might wish, more Herodotus and less Hesiod.

This little book then is a collection of aphorisms along with a few *fabulae* and musings gathered from decades. These aphorisms are often sourced from the end lines of my poems intended as summations. They also derive from my theses of various *belles lettres*, essays and book chapters. While I hope they are original and worth consideration, they may also encapsulate ideas others have thought about but articulated here in novel ways. It is hoped there are no platitudes, tendentious saws, bromides or *non sequiturs* and fallacies here, but that cannot be guaranteed. To avoid some common pitfalls, the author is greatly indebted to friends who have kindly commented or just as kindly suggested some ideas be deleted and forgotten. A few weeks well spent in London in late fall (2013) helped to refine some of these aphorisms.

Friends and mentors who have been most helpful over decades include several mathematicians such as John D. Gibbon, Emeritus Professor of Mathematics at Imperial College London; along with mathematician Rob Cook, co-founder of Pixar Studios and an Academy Award winner; also Dr. Arno Penzias (Nobel Laureate in Physics, 1978); medical doctor Dr. Katy Haynes (Oxford and London); historian Dr. Catherine Clover (D.Phil. Oxford); historian and publisher Dr. Richard Reed (D.Phil. Oxford) whose New Zealand Reed publishing family founder was knighted for services to literature and culture; archaeological scientist Dr. Dafydd Griffiths, Institute of Archaeology, University College London, University of London; Emeritus Professor of Philosophy John Perry, Stanford University; Emeritus Professor of Near Eastern Archaeology David Stronach, University of California, Berkeley; longtime mentor Cordell Hull, Dikran Karagueuzian, Publisher of the CSLI Press, Center for the Study of Language and Information, Stanford University; and other patient and worthy friends who tried to banish hubris and presumption whenever possible, although they may not have been altogether successful. Over the past half decade, James Geary, author of several magisterial books on aphorisms and metaphors,[3] now at Harvard University, has been a rowing partner in the white water rapids of the Salmon River in Idaho and a phenomenal intellectual resource when in London, whose publication of some of these aphorisms encouraged this collection.

More than any other, I owe endless gratitude to my wife Pamela, a supreme pragmatist. Despite being wakened countless times at night over almost forty years by my working through some of these aphorisms on the adjacent pillow - trying to get them right - or enduring my rising from bed in the dark to write them down, she has always remained a deep well of patience and forbearing. Truth be told, while there is no one time during day or night when ideas might wing my way, I have probably forgotten far more hundreds of attempted aphorisms in the middle of the night (having fallen asleep) than the few hundred thoughts collected here; if so, it is probable they were not worth saving. Apropos, for years I used to make weekly pilgrimages to a mentor's house, Emeritus Professor of Classics Antony Raubitschek of Stanford University, now passed into the Elysian Fields. As we would sit by the fire in his parlor, he would frequently say, ever humble, that he had hundreds of thoughts every week but usually only one of them was good enough to be worth remembering. I should be so lucky.

Patrick Hunt
2013

---

[3]   James Geary. *The World in a Phrase: A Brief History of the Aphorism*. Bloomsbury, 2005; *Geary's Guide to the World's Great Aphorists*, Bloomsbury 2007; *I is an Other: The Secret Life of Metaphor and How it Shapes the Way We See the World*, Harper Perennial repr. 2012; *All Aphorisms, All the Time* (James Geary's Blog).

Table of Contents

Aphorisms

1

"Those who are heaven-bound create a little heaven around them, those who are hell-bent make hell on earth first."

2

"Humans have stomachs twice the size of their brains and three times the size of their hearts."

3

"Angels prefer to work invisibly."

4

"Stumbling upward is a blessing in disguise."

5

"Dogs bark, foxes won't."

6

"Three million people were born the same year as Leonardo da Vinci."

7

"Fear is a monster's greatest power."

8

"Gardening may not restore innocence but makes us want to be Adam and Eve again."

9

"A cloud is one of the few things changing faster than a politician."

10

"Humans are creative because they are formed in the image of God."

11

"Even worms seek sunshine after rain."

12

"Kings are usually born but heroes are always formed."

13

"Danger is not knowing what our hands and feet are doing."

14

"Too often islands of pleasure are surrounded by oceans of pain."

15

"Gazelles and cheetahs need each other to keep sleek and fast."

16

"The will, not the body, makes the difference between the weak and the strong."

17

"Lovemaking is the closest mortals come to divinity."

18

"Faith is not irrational but suprarational."

19

"True smiles are always involuntary."

20

"Rewarding a fool is like polishing lead."

21

"Ancient Egypt knew justice should be light as a feather but injustice was an unbearable burden."

22

"Patience is an oasis in the desert of waiting."

23

"In ancient Greece, butterflies were souls on their way to Elysium."

24

"A rock resisting the stream can still end up well-rounded."

25

"Cast out your own demons before attempting anyone else's."

26

"Love and death often share the same bed."

27

"The tragedy of Beauty is its brevity."

28

"Ripples of ignorance bring about tidal waves of fear and hatred."

29

"In human contact, a hand opens for a caress or a handshake but closes for a fist or around a weapon."

30

"The secret of great saints is that they were first great sinners."

31

"Babylonian farmers knew when to harvest crops because they were ripe, but their astronomers had the more difficult task in reckoning when to plant them."

32

"Faith may be more reasonable than reason is faithful."

33

"Death is merely the vulture's brief shadow in front of the sun."

34

"Hatred is hotter than fire and colder than ice."

35

"The first dogs were wolves who realized our food tasted better than us."

36

"Sin only looks good in poor light…or in neon."

37

"Mating hyenas make love and war at the same time."

38

"Reflections of Narcissus are only seen in stagnant water."

39

"Diplomacy is too often the art of lying with a smile."

40

"Immortality is an itch we cannot scratch."

41

"A kiss is not a kiss to empty air but is like love and beauty made to share."

42

"Wine is what water dreams of becoming."

43

"Fame is for this life but glory is immortal."

44

"During Creation in the Book of Genesis when God's spirit moved across the face of the waters, the visual image is wind stirring a lake on which the sun also shines, breaking light into many reflections. The wind is only visible via light."

45

"Prophets have problems living in the present."

46

"If there is a divine purpose to everything, a mosquito is a paradox."

47

"Tyranny hates democracy because democracy offers choices."

48

"Comparing religions is like measuring moving shadows by firelight."

49

"Poets prefer ambiguities, philosophers verities."

50

"Hearing the wind is a spiritual experience."

51

"Even if we fed our souls far more than our bodies, our souls would still not be fat."

52

"Because leaves fall only once, they wait a lifetime to do it."

53

"To be loved by a dog is easy, to be loved by a cat is an achievement."

54

"Even a scorpion wants its stinging tail as far as possible from itself."

55

"If the gods invite you for a meal, be prepared for a feast of paradox."

56

"Virtue's children are nurtured, while evil abandons its children."

57

"When a tiger lets you see it, you are in danger."

58

"Unless you're a viper, visiting a den of vipers is usually quickly fatal."

59

"All galaxies we find are merely asterisks on an endless page."

60

"Even stars cast shadows before God."

61

"If death is the long sleep, life is the dream just before waking."

62

"To love the moon is folly, to be loved by the moon is lunacy."

63

"Birds don't have to talk because they can sing."

64

"Nature always balances the treasured and the toxic in metal deposition: gold comes with mercury, silver with lead and copper with arsenic."

65

"A clever fool falls headfirst."

66

"The earliest maps transformed humans into giants."

67

"The devil will always tell a little truth in order to promote a bigger lie."

68

"The only tyrannies we tolerate are those ruling our own souls."

69

"In myth, the love of a god for a human is often unbearable."

70

"God makes wings, man makes chains."

71

"The flower must die before the fruit can develop."

72

"Joy is elusive in seeking until found in giving."

73

"Praise rises, curses fall."

74

"Do cats purr more for humans than for each other?"

75

"Stars rarely light a path below but always give something higher to follow."

76

"God dances between every human heartbeat."

77

"Abbé Suger thought red and blue stained-glass windows showed spiritual tension between body and soul, he was partly right because it is optical tension between the two extremes of the visible spectrum."

78

"There are so many adders in this world because they usually don't bite each other."

79

"You can never run away from God, you can only turn away."

80

"Music is mathematics you can listen to."

81

"Age is the only thing changing gold into silver."

82

"Would that squirrels only buried acorns to grow more oaks."

83

"Only fools are enchanted by mirrors."

84

"God is the humblest being."

85

"In early Greece winners' crowns were only plants because the ancients knew victory is fleeting."

86

"Philosophers always walk more than they talk."

87

"Dance and song were the first arts."

88

"While having children makes one humble, having grandchildren makes one proud."

89

"Dreaming is for what we cannot do awake."

90

"Whoever discovered fire was burned by it first."

91

"Was Buddha's tree of enlightenment merely the richest in oxygen?"

92

"Humans build houses but worms spin silk."

93

"The language of volcanoes is always incendiary."

94

"Sand was once massive rock, rock was once a rain of stars."

95

"Praising a bore is far worse than damning a poet."

96

"The Devil's fear of heaven is rational."

97

"Giving in too much to desire is like petting a leopard."

98

"The easiest place to find wild boars is under hazelnut trees."

99

"There is no human language without a word for love."

100

"Scipio knew that many people are persuaded more by religion and the power of devotion than by reason and the power of deduction."

101

"Mountains pull our eyes upward against gravity."

102

"Faith in God is hope in certainty."

103

"You can often still see Hannibal's elephants as clouds marching over the Alps. "

104

"Plato believed beauty on earth is the glimmer of heaven."

105

"Only mortals create art out of suffering."

106

"One man's sin is another man's envy."

107

"Sleeping is temporary but dreaming is eternal."

108

"Philosophy sees green grass growing in the cracks of civilization."

109

"Anguish is proof of the soul."

110

"At day's end, the golden dream of Eldorado was just another of the sun's illusions."

111

"Moonlight makes night tolerable."

112

"Contemplating beauty makes the soul beautiful."

113

"Libraries are the greatest treasure houses in history. In them you find whole empires, endless glitter of gold and silver, armies marching to battle, mountains and jungles from which long rivers start, great cities spreading to the horizons, cathedrals and towers soaring to the sky and the thoughts that built all these or brought them to ruin."

114

"Gardening weeds out despair."

115

"How could Alexander not conquer the world? His first years with his mother told him he was a god's son; his next years with his father made him hard as iron; then his tutor Aristotle honed his adolescent mind razor sharp."

116

"Solon took law out of the wrathful grasp of the Furies."

117

"If the first will be last and the last will be first, where will the middle be but still muddling through mediocrity?"

118

"Satisfaction may not be an earthly state."

119

"Beware the embrace of a python."

120

"According to Herodotus, Cyrus was a great king because he first learned humility as a shepherd guarding his land and as a gardener cultivating his people."

121

"In old age time speeds up because we wind down."

122

"The only flowers the Devil likes are artificial."

123

"Every pantheon of deities needs a jester god."

124

"Spiders spin necklaces for dew to hang diamonds."

125

"Flies, like the damned, love the smell of corruption."

126

"Wine from Cannae is as red as Roman blood that fed the vine roots."

127

"Caves are water's long fantasies with rock."

128

"Machiavelli loved bitter almonds."

129

"Medusa's hair started out lovely."

130

"Mortality means children learn to curse before they can talk."

131

"The sound of bees predicts sweet rewards of labor."

132

"The brains of sheep contain few mysteries."

133

"A Plutarch always looks for omens after the fact."

134

"Intensity of desire is often inversely proportional to probability of attainment."

135

"The Inferno will melt lead but never be hot enough to refine gold."

136

"The Conquistadors in Mexico destroyed a civilization greater than their own."

137

"If humans were law abiding at heart, we would never need locks and keys."

138

"Night is best for lovemaking to nourish illusion in the dark."

139

"Trees cannot walk or run yet they dance with the wind."

140

"Art History should be Art as History."

141

"Stalking lions never roar."

142

"Crocodiles cannot hide their teeth when they smile."

143

"The wings of a hummingbird are small but can generate a tornado."

144

"Behavior is what you do with your eyes closed."

145

"There are three things if offered one should not turn down: dark chocolate, champagne and the last is best left unsaid."

146

"The strength of bears is matched by their weakness for honey."

147

"The most dangerous monsters are beautiful."

148

"Listening to a Siren is suicidal."

149

"Owl eyes are huge because they have to navigate in darkness."

150

"A Wasp is like a bee with a bad temper because it has nothing sweet to go home to."

151

"Intuition is the accumulation of years of experience, instinct the accumulation of eons."

152

"Stars obey the same laws as snails."

153

"Humans climb mountains to find God, ants to find food."

154

"You can chase after knowledge although wisdom will step on your toes."

155

"Elephant noses stretched into trunks and giraffe necks elongated when trees evolved to protect their lower branches."

156

"Philosopher's stones are what they put in their pockets to hold themselves down in a gale."

157

"Toes are shorter than fingers because they rarely need to cling to what they stand on."

158

"Dogs bite, cats scratch, fools talk: each is painful."

159

"Although it won't slice bread you can slice your hand on a paper's edge."

160

"The Devil can never forgive but God can."

161

"If too much ambition destroyed Caesar, perhaps not enough stopped Hannibal."

162

"Eventually the tree of youth is bent by the winds of age."

163

"Circe did not so much turn men into beasts as reveal their inner nature."

164

"Our eyes only see a small portion of the colors of flowers."

165

"Only a warthog can be beautiful to another warthog."

166

"Bach wrote music for heaven."

167

"Only leaves know the true color of sunlight."

168

"What finally unified Romans and barbarians alike in the wars against Attila and the Huns was an unprecedented nascent Christianity against paganism."

169

"Unicorns and sages drink springs at their sources."

170

"Money is a clever illusion of bankers."

171

"The colors Van Gogh saw inside his mind never faded."

172

"Unlike comets and more like candles, souls don't burn up but down."

173

"Rembrandt's women portray the most complex emotions."

174

"The simplest and oldest expression of holiness always meant 'God's property.'"

175

"Children play because their brains are growing."

176

"If only Faust knew contracts with the Devil could be broken easier than with God."

177

"Mapping dreams leads to surprising places."

178

"If war is embedded in human nature it is because we are at war with ourselves."

179

"Beelzebub was lord of the flies because he was the god of things dying."

180

"Don't be too curious to know what crows converse about."

181

"Diamonds shine because they let more light in than out."

182

"Apollo could not embrace Daphne so he made her laurel embrace him."

183

"The biggest monster Herakles fought was himself."

184

"Far better to be on the inside of the windows of Chartres."

185

"Although his body told him he was old, Goethe knew better than to grow up."

186

"If we could only invent cures as well as we do weapons."

187

"The real failure of Sisyphus was to never understand gravity."

188

"Avoid writers who hide behind more ink than a squid."

189

"Impressionism was about light, Expressionism about what light created: color."

190

"Cathedrals were intended to represent heaven on earth and yet their portals paradoxically often show judgment for the damned."

191

"Lycurgus found wisdom in economy of words."

192

"When we need lawyers rather than priests to parse the paradox of oracles, Cicero will do."

193

"The worst charlatans are the ones pretending to be holy."

194

"Etruscan banquets were so contagious even into the afterlife that they continue into Tuscan feasts today."

195

"Pride is usually either delusional or compensatory."

196

"Ask Icarus: few of Daedalus' inventions produced good results."

197

"Dragons protect their offspring too."

198

"Life is a fatal disease from which everyone dies."

199

"Learning to read people makes us wiser than only reading books."

200

"The ancients debated whether Demeter's most divine gift was grain for food or opium for pain relief."

201

"The population of Rome contains more ghosts than the living."

202

"Mutating bacteria are one of the best living evidences for evolution."

203

"Plato understood three kinds of immortality, that which belongs to the gods, another in human offspring, and the glory of heroes."

204

"Would that we have the Horn of Roland to summon angels and chase away devils."

205

"The spires of Oxford reach high because of soaring thoughts."

206

"In mathematicians' dreams, constellations are shaped like polygons."

207

"The best difference between a tool and a weapon is intent: hammers should be for construction, not destruction."

208

"We're no longer thinking when we have more answers than questions."

209

"Civilization rose because in order to survive, humans had to stick together."

210

"Mozart never had to work because he played all his life."

211

"Reincarnation offers false hope for those not inclined to get it right the first time."

212

'Fungi are one of most successful and adaptable life forms in the universe, clever enough to make many of their members indispensable to humans and plants as well as being the largest living organisms on earth, also possibly the longest living, spreading over whole forests."

213

"Wine happens when God does miracles with water."

214

"If history educates the mind, mythology instructs the soul."

215

"Gibbon's vision of Rome was as romantic as Hannibal's was toxic."

216

"Muses only inspired people who would be grateful."

217

"Wine even has its own religion."

218

"Aphrodite gives the illusion of wearing nothing but a smile."

219

"The good is the enemy of the best."

220

"Will man ever find the smallest particle in the universe?"

221

"The difference between seeing miracles without believing and believing miracles without seeing has eternal consequences."

222

"The heart of a phoenix is too hot for its body, eventually combusting."

223

"Pearls are formed by sublimating irritation."

224

"The story of old Aristotle's infatuation with the young courtesan Phyllis proves love is twice as wise as sophistry."

225

"Power is the most corrosive drink the soul could thirst after."

226

"Tales of trolls in caves may be dim memories of Neanderthals."

227

"Eve's mistake was not talking to a snake but first believing it had anything worth saying."

228

"Mendel's laws may have been inspired by reading Jacob's animal breeding scheme in Mesopotamia."

229

"The wheels of commerce have always driven civilization: writing and literature are secondary products of keeping records."

230

"One book missing from the Library of Alexandria was a study of fire brigades - Nero borrowed and never returned it."

231

"Singing vibrates the whole person, unifying every cell."

232

"Worshipping Nature rather than its Creator is like appreciating a frame more than the painting."

233

"Political Economy is too often an oxymoron."

234

"Church holy relics multiplied exponentially when it was required that each new bishopric have one."

235

"When a fool marries wisdom, he becomes wiser, yet wisdom does not become foolish."

236

"Agostino Chigi, being banker to two popes, made his treasure on earth, not heaven."

237

"It is an absurdity to think God can be exclusively claimed by any human institution."

238

"If teachers cannot learn from their students, they cannot teach them either."

239

"Fortuna is a heartless mistress, as Hannibal found; one day he bathed in glory, the next pursued as a fugitive."

240

"Centaurs were merely the first horsemen Greeks saw from a distance."

241

"Solomon - or his legend - anticipated Aristotle's natural history for several hundred years by dividing life into land beasts, birds of the air, fishy sea creatures and things that usually crawl underground."

242

"The golden apple of strife only looks sweet."

243

"Heroes in struggles expect gods, gods expect struggles in heroes."

244

"The most redemptive state anyone can know is being loved."

245

"Being honorable is the greatest wealth."

246

"The rarest flowers blossom in winter."

247

"In the right hands, a poison becomes a medicine."

248

"Librarians are the keepers of civilization."

249

"Scandal is the gospel of a society in ruins."

250

"The proud find prayer difficult because it is humbling."

251

"One small fence in the right place can prevent an avalanche."

252

"Humans looking up at the stars feel humble, but who knows what wolves feel?"

253

"Inside Lascaux and Chauvet caves you can only see the horses and aurochs run in flickering firelight."

254

"Deepest loneliness can occur in the greatest crowds of people."

255

"Some flowers in the desert wait years for rain to blossom."

256

"We love to hear fountains because since the dawn of prehistory we instinctively recognize health and life in the sound of running water."

257

"From the hare's perspective, it outruns the moon."

258

"Courage does not act necessarily in the absence of fear but in spite of it."

259

"One difference between myth and reality is that while the gods are real, we are their myths."

260

"A constellation is a village where stars live."

261

"A pity humanity has more monuments to pride than to virtue."

262

"It is far better to hang on to the last shred of hope rather than let go and fall into the abyss of despair."

263

"Socrates looked like a satyr but did not act like one, proving his external appearance did not reflect his internal character; conversely Alcibiades was a most handsome traitor."

264

"Choirs of angels drive the devil crazy with envy; this is the Lucifer Syndrome. Likewise humans who are jealous when others are praised instead of them also have the devil's malady."

265

"The insufferable gastronome should remember that a sow may love stinking mud as much as truffles."

266

"Ireland's golden mists have birthed many magical tales, gilding the imaginations and tongues of bards."

267

"Elijah was fed by ravens in the wilderness - somehow not defiled by scavenged carrion - and still ascended to heaven in a fiery chariot."

268

"The Greeks unfolded the idea that destination was the outcome of destiny."

Alexander and the Caladrius

Babylon was patiently waiting for Alexander to die, although because everyone said he was a god, it might not happen as predicted. The date palm trees of the Euphrates River stood calmly in the early summer heat along the canalized banks, the distant ones shimmering in the heat although there was no breeze from the Zagros Mountains to the east and the range was so far away no one could see its lavender hued peaks from this city of dusty brown brick.

The priests had come with endless sheep they slaughtered, peering daily into bloody entrails while Alexander tossed with fever, his brow hot and his hair damp in sweat. Legend had it that his breath had always smelled like lilies, but his doctors now only detected a whiff of foul corruption from his nostrils. At night in their towers high above the smoke and ambient lamplight of Babylon, the stargazers looked into the heavens for a sign that would tell them anything about Alexander's destiny, but the stars were inscrutable.

In their tents, the Macedonian soldiers grumbled because no one would tell them anything either. Their once-beloved Alexander had dissipated himself into a wreck, aping the Mesopotamians with their perfumes and haughtiness. They all knew Alexander's body was wracked with scars from countless battles even though it was always fully covered with glittering robes studded with gems when he had rarely appeared in public over the last year. Although so often he had charged into battle with his bare head unhelmeted, he had survived every wound that no one else could have endured.

Only a few trusted companions were at Alexander's bedside. Although they could not hear the fitful silences between his groans as the companions did, his loyal soldiers were camped outside the city far from their king. Those who had faithfully given up their youth to follow him across the world were left to wonder, completely out of any line of communication about this king who once used to talk to every one of them personally without arrogance before a battle, filling them with trust. The Macedonians thought that now there were too many oily Persian eunuchs to let anyone close to Alexander or let some truth slip about a sick king too remote for them to even glimpse.

His oldest soldiers remembered how he had tamed Bucephalus as a boy, somehow knowing the great wild horse was afraid of its own shadow. His father King Philip had said, "My son, Greece is not large enough for you." They recalled how Alexander had led the way across the Hellespont in a broad fleet of ships. Just before the keels hit the shore, the young king had thrown his spear over the waves into the sand of Asia, then jumped laughing into the surf to land first and claim the land for Greece. They had followed Alexander to Gordion where he had stood in the city square before the mathematician's famous knot. Oracles had said, "Whoever looses this knot will conquer Asia." Alexander examined the knot no one could untie, and then took a novel approach. His soldiers had watched as Alexander pulled out his sword and slashed through the famous giant knot, fulfilling the oracle in his own inimitable way.

Alexander had led them to the Battles at Issus and Gaugamela where Darius had fled with his thousands of men. His soldiers were awestruck how he had himself planned and built the stone causeway out to sea to conquer the proud coastal island of Tyre. They saw him stagger half-dead with thirst ahead of them in the burning sand to the Siwa oasis of Amun's shrine in Egypt. They had been amazed at the immense wealth of Persia and after chasing the Persian king for years, they were silenced when Alexander wept at the mangled dying Darius on the Oxus River and had given him an emperor's burial. They had even followed their king to the jungles of India and heard the dozens of war elephants trumpeting before battle. Desperate for water, they had later watched with parched throats and swollen tongues as Alexander poured out the single helmet full of water they saved for him in the Gedrosian desert, saying he could not drink only for himself if no one else could. These who had survived all this were the same soldiers who had nearly worshipped Alexander, for who else could have conquered the world? Now his soldiers knew the conqueror was paying for all his incredible feats, having ignored lifelong what mortality was left in his worn and broken body.

At Alexander's bedside, the Babylonian, Persian and even Greek doctors had done everything they could, but nothing improved Alexander's steadily sinking condition over more than a week. Whether marsh fever, poison from old wounds or the overall toll on his body, nobody could fathom the depth of his sickness and only those by his bedside saw his once golden locks were now prematurely edged with dingy gray. In his early thirties he looked much older than his years. Even those high officers who despised Alexander shuddered to see how a god waned to mortality.

Someone in the court had spent a lot of gold to bring rare phoenix feathers from China over the highest mountains in the world of eternal snows. They burned the phoenix feathers to ash in a brazier before Alexander thinking it might also cause him to rise from the embers of fever but he only coughed in the smoke without waking, his breath raspy. Alexander's eyes had not opened in days and in the same time he had not said a discernible word, although his cracked lips moved once in awhile. One or another of his generals would then bend down to listen wanting to be the mediator to the others but no sound escaped his lips. Rare almug wood from India was also burned for its fragrant charcoal that would relieve catarrh, but this had no effect either other than to fill Alexander's bedroom with choking vapors, and the windows had to be opened, as they remained.

Another Persian had gone to the garden palace of Cyrus and cut down a precious old citron tree with its exotic fruit, trying to revive the king with the flesh and juice of this tree said to be a marvelous medical remedy for any ailment. This too had no effect other than to dismay the elder officers of highest rank because Alexander was more and more unconscious to the world. No one knew what else to do and everyone in the room dreaded telling the Macedonian soldiers Alexander was dying.

That was when the fabled caladrius bird flew into the open window all the way from the far off Elbruz Mountains, folding its white wings as it sat down at the king's bedside. Only the wisest Persians and Babylonians recognized what it was, and they gasped.

"The caladrius has come, all on its own!"

They knew the significance of this magical bird, the caladrius that lived almost above the clouds of high Mt. Demavand. This was the same feathered creature that the precursor of Noah - the immortal Utnapishtim - in the Epic of Gilgamesh and later the newer scriptures let out of his boat after the Flood, but it had not returned except every few hundred years in a prophetic task to the bedside of sick kings. The Persians and Babylonians went very quiet to see what the caladrius would do. At first it did nothing but preen its feathers, not once turning its head toward the king.

The legends said that if the caladrius would look upon a sick king, he would revive and live. The bird had the power to draw out from a sick king all his disease and illnesses regardless of how fatal. But if the caladrius never looked at a sick king, he would surely die.

Then the caladrius stopped preening and listened on its bedside perch. The Persians and Babylonians held their breath and the Greeks did too, thinking this was the proper thing. A fly wandered into the room through the open window, possibly drawn by the bad smell of feverish sweat. It buzzed by the bed and the caladrius bird with one orange eye swiftly tracked and snatched it out of the air with its beak, swallowing it quickly. But the white bird settled back and still did not look at the king. Toward afternoon it tucked its head in its wing and slept, never moving from its bedpost while the king's breath was rough in his throat. The caladrius bird awoke before sunset, stretching one wing and then grew very still. The king's breath was now labored, as if every intake burned. All this time the caladrius bird had never looked over at Alexander's face, never even glancing toward the king's body on the bed where it sat.

The group of close advisors, generals and doctors had hardly moved for hours, some dozing, others afraid of upsetting the bird. Finally all noticed that Alexander's breathing was becoming shorter and shorter, sounding more and more painful as if his chest was being crushed in a vice. His face was pale as snow but hot as a glowing ember. Then everyone heard the long, low last breath of the world's conqueror. Alexander's inward sigh was longer than anyone would have thought to count and then he exhaled to the softest whisper breaking like a wave on a distant shore until there was nothing left. Only then in silence did the great caladrius turn and knowingly look one long sad gaze at the dead king. Finally it spread its wings and flew out the window into the darkening purple dusk.

The Museum of Ordinary Objects

There is a tiny museum in London so secret almost no one knows about it. It has no open hours or uninvited visitors. Its location is most carefully guarded and it is hidden on a back street within the buried walls of the former Roman city of old Londinium and almost as deep below the streets. You could pass by its undistinguished door and never know it. The museum is reached after descending hundreds of steps and it is only one small room, not brightly lit. Those rare persons who have been invited one at a time never talk about what four small objects they have seen there, but they vividly remember this museum.

Because the room is underground, there are no windows. The objects are displayed on a rickety wooden table in dim light from a bare light bulb hanging below the ceiling. The first object is a small moldy animal tail in bad condition. The second object is a rusty iron needle. The third object is a piece of broken obsidian. The fourth and final object is a faded rag with a patchwork image. The objects did not belong to anyone important. No king, queen or emperor owned them, no great hero or general touched them, and no pope or high priest blessed them. They are the humblest, most ordinary objects possible, yet they have great significance. Despite their condition, a brief description of these ordinary objects in no chronological order contrasts hugely with the momentous events they witnessed in history.

The first object in the museum is a small moldy animal tail. On close inspection it can be identified as a rat tail, with only a few hairs left near its base. It came from Alexandria about the year 537 when Constantinople with its golden domes ruled mighty Byzantium. Here Justinian was emperor over an almost endless land and great ships sailed from the Bosporus and the Golden Horn to Alexandria and back for pearls, silk and spices out of the glorious East.

Two years before had been a crop disaster. Fruit froze on trees and many never saw the sun through a cloudy haze even in Anatolia. Far away, Chinese scribes recorded from their vast trade empire that massive volcanoes had spewed ash and dust down in Java the prior year and Chinese scientists even suggested the connection between the dim light and agricultural failures.

"We do not think this is due to an unlucky conjunction of the stars. We think there might be a link between the volcanoes at the edge of the world and our darkened sky and lack of a growing season," they told the emperor as they bowed.

All over the vastness of the Asian continent people were going hungry from insufficient food. It was the old cycle of the Four Horsemen of the Apocalypse – famine, disease, war and death – although at first only the early stages began to appear.

The famine in Byzantium weakened the health of the populace. When plague first took its early victims in

Alexandria, few knew it had come down the Nile from tropical Africa. As usual, rats crawled up the ropes of ships docked at Alexandria's bustling port and they also carried fleas infected with pestilence. Long before the dead began to pile up in Alexandria, the ships had already reached Constantinople and the plague spread silently without regard to wealth or station across the harbor and hills of the capital city.

But soon the wails of the dying drowned out the bells of churches across Constantinople, Chora and all the ports where the rats had spread the unstoppable disease, hundreds of rats dying themselves along the wharves and in the city streets. Without even knowing the role of the rats in spreading the plague, someone had long ago saved this little remnant of a rat tail to remind how pervasive the plague was that it even brought rats out of the sewers to die in daylight, since rats normally kept out of sight in darkness. At the height of the plague corpses were left unburied and while many prayed, an equal number cursed. A few flagellating anchorite monks blamed the plague on sex because the dark purple lumps affected the groin most.

"God is punishing your fleshly desires," the anchorites harangued.

When the ravages of plague were finally tapering off, the great city of Constantinople and all its outposts across Byzantium were ghosts of themselves. Where hordes of traders had filled the marketplaces, noisy and bustling with rich goods, footsteps now rang hollow on the empty squares. The sun had returned, shining again on the golden domes, but the population was devastated. The voice of one surviving historian, Procopius, counted that in a few years the city of Constantinople had shrunk from 500,000 residents to 300,000, and this same loss was reflected across the whole of Byzantium. By the year 600 almost half the once thriving population was gone. No family had been spared from death and whole neighborhoods had been wiped out by the plague that had quickly followed the famine across the empire. There was a great loss of strength across the outposts of Anatolia, a vacuum of leadership and power in the Near East where Byzantium had ruled for centuries.

"We have no soldiers to place in the outpost guardhouses at the edge of empire," the generals told the Byzantine court, "Hardly enough to even fully field the imperial guards here in Constantinople."

Then only two decades later to the south in the desert of Arabia, a new prophet appeared and soon his fiery message and the fierce sword of Islam followed in a stampede of devotion sweeping across the Near East. Many shrines and churches of Byzantium across the Holy Land were swallowed up in the tide of change, converted into mosques with minarets piercing the sky. Not only was Alexandria where the rats appeared first but also one of the first cities to fall to Islam. The vacuum left by famine and plague in Byzantium was filled by the new power. Much of this change was made possible by a geographical logic, wherever rat feet had first clambered in dark and hidden places until plague festered openly in the light. A rat tail preserved in the museum was a token of the earthshaking changes and alignments that followed the rats of Alexandria through the whole of Byzantium. The moldy rat tail in the museum looks so small and weak, but its message is powerful as its role came to be understood. Who can predict what small things might have such a large impact on history?

The museum's second object under a dim light is the rusty iron needle. It came out of a battlefield, brought by a weary soldier from the blood-soaked battlefield in what is now Champagne, France. At the Battle of Chalons in 452, the ferocious Huns had finally gathered like a dark storm on the horizon, racing on their horses from the steppes of the east with their new allies, the equally pagan Scythians. Attila, the Scourge of God, had taken the invitation from Honoria, the western emperor's traitorous sister who wanted her freedom, and he now demanded both his bride and the entire land.

On their way west, the Huns raped innumerable women, ransacked scores of churches and beheaded bishops and parishioners alike, impaling their heads on ruined walls. Since their manhood could not be proven without a grisly victim, many of the Huns and Scythians wore human skin trophies stretched across their shields and human skulls rattled on their saddles like gourds. Hordes of carrion birds followed their armies across the sky, darkening the sun. The Huns' cruel bows could be armed and shot from moving horseback, volleys of arrows arcing across a field long before their spears and swords were bloodied.

The diminished and tottering West had to meet the challenge of Attila or completely fall to the pagan barbarians. Only one general, Aetius, could be counted to fight and he had nowhere near enough forces to match Attila. Christianity was new to many of the people allied in the West, and since Aetius was a Roman after all, people now barely within the margins of the changed Roman world like the Burgundians and Lombards still hated Rome. At first these Burgundian and Lombard clans refused to fight with Aetius against the Huns who had long crossed the Rhine and were assembling to the north in the rolling Champagne country. While Attila was ravaging the north unchecked, it wasn't until a brave bishop persuaded the new tribes that it was their Christian duty to face the pagan Huns and Scythians.

"You are Christians now," the bishop pleaded. "This is the first real threat we have together faced as Christian peoples. We are no longer merely Burgundians, Lombards and Romans but a people who serve God. The Huns will kill all of us with the same rage if we do not join together under the Cross. We can only pray that God may reward our new unity."

The allied tribal chiefs argued at first but at last comprehended this new identity and agreed to overcome their old distrust of Rome and join Aetius. They marched quickly toward the besieged fort city of Orleans and relieved it as the Huns left eastward, preparing to meet the Roman allied forces at Chalons. The Romans knew the dire reputation of Attila and his formidable army of mounted horses, prickling with wicked barbed weapons and howling like wolves in battle, a frightening combination that could turn the hearts of hardened soldiers cold with fear.

At Chalons a young priest had with him a tattered relic, a woven standard of the sign of Christ in the Chi-Rho made of linen and embroidered with silk, but it was hundreds of years old and could hardly survive being carried into battle, almost threadbare with some of its weave barely intact. The anonymous priest had a last desperate idea the night before the full battle when the Christian soldiers muttered by their campfires, many drinking anything to bolster their spirits and catch a little sleep mostly haunted by fear.

The priest began to unravel the entire cloth relic, warp by woof, and took it around the entire army on the front wherever the troops would face the furious charges of Attila. He showed the consecrated object and told them it was a blessed relic before he snipped a small hanging thread for each soldier. With a small iron needle the priest then stitched one short piece of holy thread to the armor of each man until he had thus equipped the entire front several rows deep and there was nothing left of the cloth relic, finishing at dawn. Exhausted but reciting scripture to each man, he exhorted them that they had some better, more powerful protection against the pagans.

"You have now put on the Armor of God," he preached.

When battle broke in a few hours, the Huns came charging with hoarse war screams to their pagan gods under a crimson sun with the black crows rising with dread wings behind them for the kill. But each Roman and new ally at the front had his confidence somehow bolstered with a new hope in protection from a holy thread sewn to his armor. The army of Rome held ground and resisted the multiple charges of Attila's frightening army. Not demoralized, the Romans and allies held their shields close together and thrust their spears outward until the mobile units of Aetius' cavalry could sweep around the line to meet the Huns from the rear and draw them away.

The battle resulted in horrible losses for the Romans but equally devastating for the Huns, who finally retreated east when they could not break through the Roman and allied lines. Even the priest was killed along with many wars leaders and countless soldiers on each side. But the iron needle was found and saved and with it the story how Christendom was saved. The needle and the relic may not have been as important as the fact that because the Romans held, the Huns abandoned their holocaust in the West. If faith was found by enough soldiers to fight against the specter of a fearsome enemy, the role of the little iron needle need not be ignored as the agency of spreading courage, always needed in whatever battle humans fight against evil of any kind under whatever banner.

The third object in the museum is a piece of broken Mexican obsidian. It was mined from under the volcanoes of the valley around Lake Texcoco where the great Aztec city of Tenochtitlan prospered in the middle of the lake. In 1519 Cortez came with his small band of conquistadors from Spain, riding warhorses and pulling their cannons on wooden carts. Allies among the enemies of the Aztecs also accompanied the few hundred conquistadors. When they rode down out of the ring of mountains into the lake valley and saw the city of Tenochtitlan before them, the armored soldiers marveled at a city filled with gardens, running fresh water and streets paved with stone, knowing Seville and Toledo only had stone laid down in the principal plazas. Back in Spain one had to be careful walking to avoid the smelly slop of poured chamber pots.

The first Aztecs to see the mounted conquistadors thought horse and man were one fused beast.

"Why do these soldiers never bathe?" the people of Mexico wondered. "They stink worse than animals."

Smallpox brought by the conquistadors also took a great toll on Mexico's native peoples. The botanically astute Aztecs gave the visitors freely of their chocolate, beans, avocadoes, tomatoes and bounty until they became wary of Cortez's masquerade as an avatar of their god Fathered Serpent. On the other hand, the Spanish were shocked at the hard religion of the Aztecs and its bloodthirsty gods, calling it a devil's creed. Whether looking for reasons to rationalize the destruction of a culture or if conversion of Mexico was possible, Christian priests wrote tracts back and forth debating about the fate of the people of the New World.

"Do they even have souls?" one theologian asked.

The Spaniards were most greedy for the gold of Eldorado, and while the Aztecs were astonished the conquistadors didn't revere green jade as they did, the destiny of the city and the Aztec empire were ultimately decided by cannon and gunpowder and armor and the cunning of Cortez, always outnumbered by the eagle and jaguar warriors of Mexico but never overwhelmed by obsidian weapons that could chop off an arm with one slice if armor did not protect it. The piece of obsidian in the museum was from an Aztec stone axe that shattered when it struck Spanish steel, sharp but brittle as the civilization that carved it.

One fateful night in 1520 named *La Noche Triste*, Night of Sorrows, under a barrage of obsidian spears and axes, the embattled conquistadors fled with boatloads of heavy gold, most of which sank and dumped their contents in the lake, likely never retrieved. No one knew how Moctezuma had been killed, whether at the hands of the Spaniards or his own Mexica peoples. Soon afterward the city of Tenochtitlan was destroyed and its temples and marketplaces razed. Its stone streets were filled with rubble and its aqueducts clogged. A proud civilization came crashing down, never renewed and the suffering people of Mexico took on the mantle of a new creed whose savior also suffered like them. But the broken piece of obsidian blade the destruction of Tenochtitlan reminds of how mighty civilizations can rise and fall in a matter of generations. In one day a Mexican or Peruvian king can become a slave in chains. The question remains whether the greater civilization won or lost. Even jagged obsidian that can easily slice open a rib cage may be superseded as a symbol of frightening power. No civilization or culture is impervious.

The museum's fourth object is a faded rag of a yellow patch. It came from Paris near the end of a terrible war. It is a Star of David, worn by a French Jew until the Liberation of Paris in the summer of 1944. When the French Resistance in Paris realized the Nazis were losing their grip on Paris in late July and early August, they began concerted efforts to accelerate the end of Nazi control. The Resistance was infuriated when the last convoy train to Buchenwald concentration camp left with 2,600 Jews on August 15, dragged out of a makeshift Paris prison despite Resistance efforts to stop further atrocities. This deportation happened in the northeastern Pantin suburb, the same place the Nazis had entered Paris in summer of 1940. Much of France was shamed by the Vichy collaboration in the south and finally had enough.

The Resistance responded that day with a general strike that spread from the workers of the Paris Metro to the Gendarmerie and police; postal workers joined the strike the next day. The Gestapo amped up the pressure by luring 35 members of the Resistance to the Bois de Boulogne park, and killing them all by the waterfall with machine guns and grenades until they were mostly beyond recognition. Hitler had told the Nazi leadership to inflict maximum damage and destroy Paris with explosives rather than let it fall to the Resistance and into the hands of the advancing Allies who were approaching from the west. Hitler's missals raged to his occupying army about to leave that they were not to spare one historic monument.

"Blow up every bridge. Leave that ungrateful Paris a pile of rubble and ash. Nothing is to be left standing. Starve the people of Paris."

On August 19 a huge barge packed with mines exploded in Pantin, destroying the windmills that had made flour from grain for the city food supply for years, following Hitler's orders.

Many Parisians now openly joined the Resistance and built barricades all over the city, greatly limiting Nazi mobility on August 20. The Nazis were unable to destroy the city because of the 20,000 Resistance members and their growing ranks of citizens who were emboldened by the approaching Allies along with the ranks of gendarmes and city police and who refused to cooperate. The Nazis pulled back and columns of their tanks, trucks and convoy vehicles began to exit the heart of Paris along the Champs Élysées, leaving only their garrisons around major city monuments. The Resistance now controlled the rest of Paris and its members were putting up posters everywhere asking free French to help liberate the city. That week over 800 French Resistance fighters were killed and another 1500 were wounded in open skirmishes as Nazi power crumbled.

On August 24 the French 2nd Armored Division raced east and entered an unguarded Paris against the orders of the Allied Command but to the cheers of thousands of Parisians who collected in the streets to celebrate. During the night the Nazis had mainly evaporated, some fleeing east from the city but 2,700 were captured and held. The remaining Nazi Command surrendered on August 25 at the Hotel Meurice but many of their snipers were still hiding across the roofs of city monuments they had held, including near the Place de la Concorde where crowds were gathering to await the victory parade of General de Gaulle on August 26 down the Champs Élysées.

One French Jew had hidden and escaped out of the Pantin Gestapo prison, a former gendarmerie office for the neighborhood. This happened during the chaos and the rushed order for final collection on the last train to Buchenwald because the Nazis were in such a hurry. He had remained hidden for days but finally risked his safety to join the throng near the Hotel Crillon where General de Gaulle would soon pass by. Emaciated but full of anticipation, he was still wearing his coat with the yellow Star of David. Sniper fire from at least one hidden Nazi on the roof of the Hotel de Crillon had earlier scared the crowd on the thoroughfare but had gone silent.

The Jew had arrived and stood under a tree below the Hotel de Crillon but no one had spotted the last invisible Nazi sniper of a few hours earlier. A minute before the hand picked guards of General Gaulle marched forward in line into plain view of the sniper, this Jew who had escaped Buchenwald was savoring his freedom and the joy of the French crowd. Suddenly he fathomed the sniper's real intention and warned a few members of the Resistance who had arms. But he didn't tell them his full plan. Half a minute before the Free French troops arrived into the open space between trees with a marching band for General de Gaulle who would pass by exactly here, this half-starved Jew ran out into the open, waving his arms, exposing his yellow star in plain view of all and shouting as loudly as possible to attract the attention of the sniper.

"Look, I'm a Jew, I'm a Jew," he danced and shouted, pointing to his Star of David. He stopped moving to face the hotel. "You can't kill all of us." The Jew taunted the sniper into firing at least a round, knowing the Nazi would be enraged and couldn't hold back from years of toxic propaganda that had fostered mindless hatred. Expertly aimed sniper bullets struck the Jew in a dozen places and he fell dying, his blood pooling on the pavement. But the Resistance lost their momentary shock and noted the revealed position of the last sniper. Thanks to the Jew, some of them had earlier entered the Hotel de Crillon and were already searching quickly. The shouts of their pointing comrades and the sounds of gunfire led them to the hiding place and with a roar they killed the last Nazi sniper who had given away his position. The dead French Jew's eyes were open, looking upward. He died knowing he had saved General de Gaulle's life because he had correctly guessed that was the sniper's real target. His body was gently removed just before the marching band arrived. The Hotel de Crillon kindly paid for his burial and his yellow star was saved as a treasure for all time, a nameless ordinary man whose sacrifice should be remembered.

The museum was set up so the invited ones might learn and never forget each object's importance. No one knows if or when they will receive an invitation to this museum, but the invitation will eventually come to presidents, prime ministers and the like persons who wield enormous power and influence. These leaders are the ones meant to learn how important ordinary objects used by common people can change the world. The invited are meant to leave much humbler. This museum of ordinary objects teaches those who choose to lead to never underestimate how history can turn on a moment. If the leaders leave without learning or later forget, they are not likely to be remembered for much that is positive.

But the rat tail, rusty iron needle, piece of obsidian and the yellow star rag are not what is important in the museum of ordinary objects. It is the extraordinary lesson of how the apparently mundane objects and people are the backbone of history. Ironically, it is only the few leaders who need to see the museum objects and remember because the rest of the world, the humble ordinary folk, already know these truths.

The Wine of Rilke

In the Grison Alps the Benedictine monks of Pfäfers began planting wine grapes in the upper Swiss Rhine valley in the tenth century. The high mountains cast long shadows over the valley but also shielded the vines from cold winds. The medieval vineyards faced toward Italy not far to the south where the warm foehn wind not only kept the snows from being deep but also melted them early. Hot springs also bubbled at the junctions of rugged mountain rock near valley floor. The monastery novices thought this was the most beautiful place on earth.

"Trust me," the chief viticulturist monk said, his white head uncovered above his habit because it was still warm during September evenings under the alpenglow. "I've surveyed all the valley for leagues and this is the sunniest spot." History proved him right as later connoisseurs still often confuse the wines of this alpine valley in the Bündner-Herrschaft with the prized Chambolle-Musigny of famous Burgundy far to the west.

The hot springs eventually became the picturesque resort spa of Bad Ragaz, suitably elegant and charming for the rich who came in their horse carriages and then by train and eventually by chauffeured motorcars.

But the old winery of the monks was replanted in the seventeenth century by the scions of a noble family of Chur in the Grisons, the genteel von Salis line who were bishops and lords. They built a great Baroque castle in 1604 looking over the town of Maienfeld and soon planted a willow tree, since the *Salix* (willow) was the emblem of their heraldry. One of the von Salis daughters, Hortensia, loved books and learning and became a scholar and defender of rights even before she married Rudolf Gugelberg von Moos and inherited the great house. She had written letters to her bishop cousins in Chur that defended wise women accused of being witches.

"These women only used the same plant medicines the monks of Pfäfers recorded years ago from Dioscorides on their vellum manuscripts," she wrote. "I've seen these books in the monks' library. So be with me on the side of justice." Hortensia's father had been the noble advocate and guardian of justice in Maienfeld and he had raised her to be articulate in a man's world. Her bishop cousins were afraid to argue with her.

Her family built a torkel, a winery barrel room, attached to the house where the date "1658" was painted over the huge wooden door. Hortensia loved to sit and read under the peaceful willow with her back to its trunk. In a gentle breeze the tree would move and she could feel it bend against her back as if it was dancing in the wind. The willow tree grew and lasted for hundreds of years by the gate above the vineyard.

In 1799, after a lifetime of fighting everyone from Ottoman Turks to Napoleon, the erudite Marshal Alexander Suvorov of Russia was forced to retreat in winter through the steepest passes of the Alps with a destitute army, quipping, "I am following Hannibal unwillingly." Suvorov stayed at this castle, a guest of the grateful von Gugelberg family as he saved the great house from certain destruction by marauding armies passing through the valley who hacked down vines for firewood. One surprisingly warm afternoon when the bench had been cleared of traces of snow, Suvorov sat in oblique sunlight under the spreading willow tree and read his well-worn copy of Plutarch.

Many dignitaries continued visiting during summer to the great house in Maienfeld for visits when passing through between Germany and Italy, friends of either the von Salis family in Chur or now married into the Gugelberg von Moos cousins in Maienfeld, where the great house was now named Schloss Salenegg, every bit an elegant Swiss manor castle with Rococo touches now embellishing the Baroque architecture. One of the von Salis cousins, Johann von Salis-Seewis, was a poet in Chur and knew Goethe and Schiller. Some of his poems were even set to music by Franz Schubert. He brought Goethe and Schiller to the house in Maienfeld and they too sat by the willow tree and talked about the mountains towering overhead while sipping the house wine. The willow now shaded the courtyard facing the valley. When the poets would talk, the long slender branches of the mature willow would weave dappled sunlight around them. This, the oldest continuous vineyard in Europe, had its replanting over the centuries renewed with different grapes, but had for hundreds of years shared the same soil by the house with the widening roots of the great willow.

Just after the first World War the poet Rainer Maria Rilke came through Maienfeld, and he stayed some weeks as a guest at Schloss Salenegg, the von Gugelberg castle, while recuperating from severe illness, since poets had always been welcome. His health had always been fragile and he had little energy. Only in his forties, he had been told he had less than six months to live. By this time the old willow had gradually lost all its branches and its dried out huge trunk had been cut down, leaving only a dead stump.

Rilke was trying to write his *Orpheus* sonnets but was too tired to do anything but observe as he sat on a bench where warm sun reflected off the wall. Rilke watched as some of the grape lees from red wine production were poured out of a small barrel placed on the willow stump. The dark lees stained the top of the willow stump and leaked down through cracks until the dry wood had absorbed all the juice. Rilke reflected on the willow and a line of poetry eventually came to him: *He can best weave the willow branches who has lived among its roots.* Rilke spent many of the days of his visit sitting in the same warm courtyard spot. A week later, as he was coming out into the courtyard through the house, he heard the surprised voice of one of the vineyard coopers by the tree stump.

"That willow tree was dead for years, but I swear it has sprouted again. Look at this new shoot." He gestured to an approaching coworker and Rilke hurried over to see too. "I wonder what caused this?" the cooper asked, searching around the stump with its tender new green shoot.

"Look at the wine stain here, it's faded but fairly fresh." The other cooper ventured. "Remember we put that small barrel here about six days ago and emptied out the dregs. The wine and lees even seeped down into the wood. I bet that's what did it. But I have no idea how or why."

"Well, if this is what our wine does to a dead tree, I should drink more of it," the first cooper laughed.

Rilke thought a lot about it for a few days, watching the willow regenerate before his eyes. Being a somewhat religious man, he intuitively called it a resurrection. Maybe this wine could also do wonders for him, he pondered. He asked for a bottle of the Salenegg wine from the cellars and drank one glass a day for his last week in Maienfeld. He wasn't surprised when he began to feel just a little better each day. He even wrote a full sonnet about the resurrection wine, giving the handwritten manuscript to Baron von Gugelberg. On leaving, Rilke asked for and paid for a case to be shipped to his residence in west Switzerland's Chateau Muzot, where he quickly finished his *Duino Elegies* collection of poetry with more energy than he had known in years, "a savage creative storm."

Schloss Salenegg was thrilled about the revived willow tree but while the von Gugelberg family didn't directly rename the wine after Rilke, they did supply the poet for the next few years with the requested "resurrection wine" as his health was better than in many years. His doctor even noted the difference, as

Rilke's heart was stronger. Rilke happily told him what had happened to the revived willow tree at Maienfeld.

"Just like a poet," the doctor laughed. "If this blauburgunder wine you're drinking is so restorative, that must be your secret. Perhaps the wine has prolonged your life like it revived the tree."

Rilke also quickly finished the second half of his *Orpheus* sonnets and many other poems. One of the lines of his cycle of Orpheus poems read: *mortal heart eager to press our fruit into deathless wine of endless years*. But this was not to be. Three years later Rilke's health was impacted by a new malady and he went into a sanatorium above Lake Geneva at Territet where he could overlook Montreux and the Alps of the Rocher de Nave. Some days eagles circled down from the dramatic peaks when the afternoon sun reflected off the lake. Although he was never able to return to Maienfeld, Rilke continued his correspondence as long as he could with the von Gugelberg family along with his fellow writers, musicians and artists.

When Rilke finally died a few years later of leukemia, he was buried near his Muzot home in Veyras in the Rhone Valley of Switzerland. A small Rilke monument was made at Raron, near Visp under the Alps. The von Gugelberg family put Rilke's letters into the family library of the Salenegg castle for a few decades until the Rilke Archive in Weimar amiably requested the correspondence for posterity. The Baron kept back one letter and Rilke's handwritten sonnet to the family as a legacy for his new granddaughter Helene.

He made a copy of the sonnet and sent that to Weimar too, keeping the original. He was proud of his granddaughter as she gave every sign of the same intelligence as her ancestress Hortensia whose Baroque portrait graced the great hall. Plus Helene had a knack for plants and a green thumb, so the vineyards would become second nature for her.

For both whimsy and family pride, the Baron also kept the same small barrel replenished with wine and had some of it ceremonially poured as a libation every year unto the willow stump that had regenerated. This annually coincided with the time Rilke had visited and the family's secret name for the special cuvee of "resurrection wine" was Rilke's Wine. Very little of the wine ever makes it outside Switzerland because the exclusive resort of Bad Ragaz across the valley always buys up so much of the wine release, saying it is restorative for many ills and it has become part of their health regimen. The sommeliers are proud of the wine's finesse but the resort's new doctors even claim research shows this special wine cleans the arteries and dissolves plaque from the bloodstream better than anything else they can recommend. Everybody in the alpine region of the Grisons always agrees it must be the wine of poets. Underground the invisible new willow roots mingle with the old vine roots in the western vineyard just below the castle. Each vintage does seem to be inspired.

www.ingramcontent.com/pod-product-compliance
Lightning Source LLC
Chambersburg PA
CBHW030346030726
47499CB00003B/933